To Bonté Rebekah,
born 1·8·00
With love from
Grandpa & Grandma
x   x

To Bonté Rebekah,
born 1·8·00

With love from

A BOOK OF
Promises

Elizabeth Laird ❖ *Illustrated by Michael Frith*

www.dk.com

LONDON • NEW YORK • SYDNEY • STUTTGART

The world is big out there, little one,
so put your hand in mine.

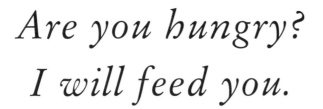

Are you hungry?
I will feed you.

If you're cold, I will warm you.

If you're sick, I will nurse you.

And if you meet with troubles, great or small,
I'll stand by you, come what may.

When you speak,
I will listen.

When you offer me gifts,
I will thank you.

When you do well, I will praise you.

If perils and dangers come near you,
I'll stand by your side,
and battle them away.

And if you're frightened of a nameless dread,
I'll hold you in my arms and protect you.

*I promise that I will
never harm you,
or threaten you,
or frighten you.*

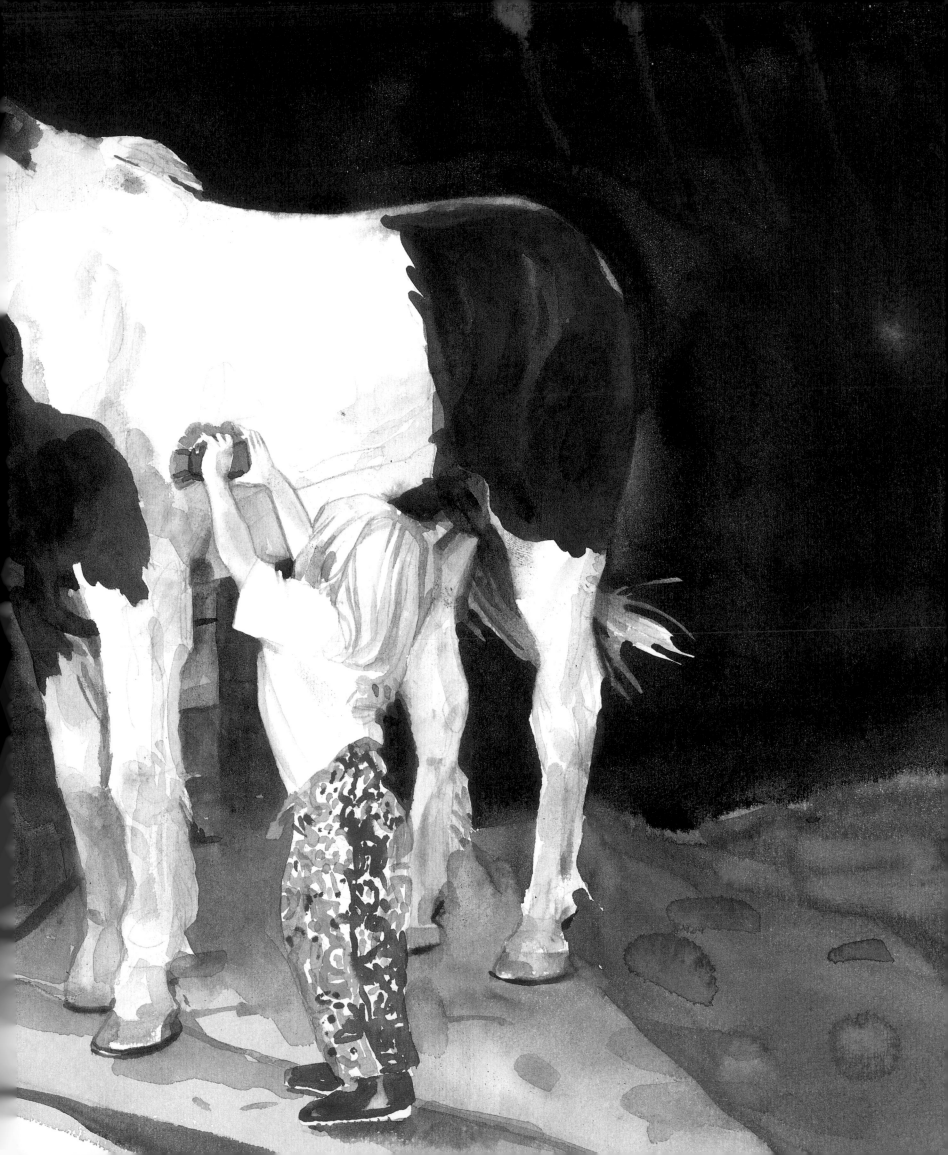

And if you should ever do me wrong,
I'll try my best to forgive you.

When you're sad,
I'll cry with you.
When you're happy,
I'll laugh with you.

I'll show you where beauty is,
and we'll walk there together.

And when all the promises are made,
there's still one more.
I promise that I'll love you,
whatever may befall.

For Molly
E.L.
For Frieda
M.F.

www.dk.com

First published in Great Britain in 1999
by Dorling Kindersley Limited,
9 Henrietta Street, London WC2E 8PS

A CIP catalogue record for this book is available from the British Library.

ISBN 0 7513 7434 2

Colour reproduction by Colourscan, Singapore
Printed and bound in Spain by Artes Gráficas Toledo, S.A.U.
D.L. TO: 1239 - 1999